There Was An Old GIANT Who Swallowed A Clock

Becky Davies

Elina Ellis

LiTTLE TiGER

LONDON

Meow

8:14

12 : 45

There was an old giant, who swallowed a **clock**,
He had a shock when he swallowed that clock!

Tick-tock,
tick-tock.

There was an old giant, who swallowed his **knitting**,
All in one sitting he swallowed his knitting!

He swallowed his knitting to muffle the clock,
He had a shock when he swallowed that clock!

Meow

There was an old giant, who swallowed some **moths**,
Which fluttered and flapped and gobbled up cloth.

He swallowed the moths to munch through his knitting,
All in one sitting he swallowed his knitting!

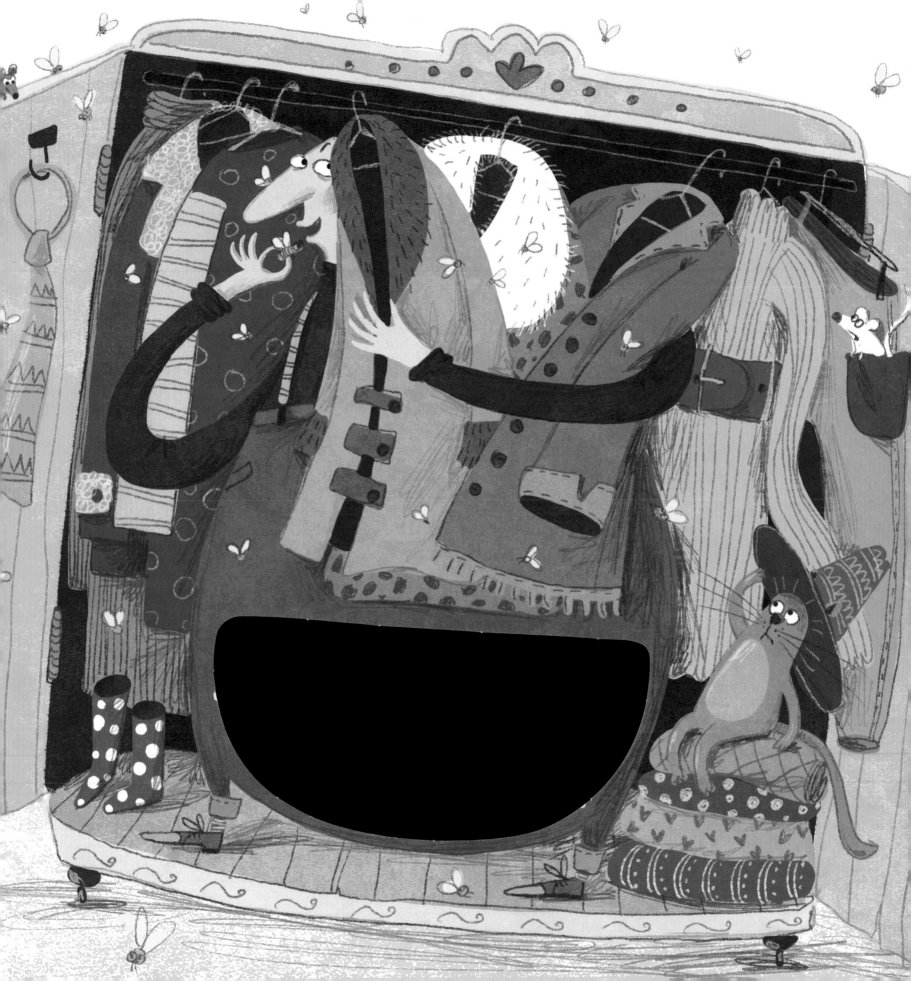

There was an old giant, who swallowed some *honey*,
Which slid down inside him, all gooey and runny.

He swallowed the honey to trap the moths,
Which fluttered and flapped and gobbled up cloth.

There was an old giant, who swallowed a **bear**,
I do declare that he swallowed a bear!

He swallowed the bear to eat up the honey,
Which slid down inside him, all gooey and runny.

There was an old giant, who swallowed a **net**,
He will regret that he swallowed that net.

He swallowed the net to catch the bear,
I do declare that he swallowed a bear!

There was an old giant, who swallowed a **boat**,
Which wouldn't go down and got stuck in his throat.

He swallowed the boat to pull in the net,
He will regret that he swallowed that net!

There was an old giant, who swallowed the *sea*,
Not very clever I'm sure you'll agree!

He swallowed the sea to wash down the boat,
Which wouldn't go down and got stuck in his throat.

There was an old giant who swallowed a – *wait!*

He gasped as he floated away from his plate!

Up from the table and into the sky, higher and higher, *impossibly high!*

Up went the giant and with him the **sea**, up went the sea, and with it the **boat**,

Up went the boat, and with it the **net**, up went the net, and with it the **bear**,

Up went the bear, and with it the **honey**, up went the honey, and with it the **moths**,

Up went the moths, and with them the **knitting**,

Up went the knitting, and with it the **clock**,

Because his big belly was full of **moon rock!**